This book belongs to

....

Sir J. M. Barrie

was born in Scotland in 1860.
He wrote many plays during his lifetime,
and *Peter Pan*, published in 1904,
was originally written for the stage.
He turned it into a novel,
Peter Pan and Wendy, seven years later.

———————

Retold by Joan Collins
Illustrated by George Buchanan
Woodcuts by Jonathan Mercer

Cover illustration by Carol Newsom

Published by Ladybird Books Ltd
80 Strand London WC2R 0RL
A Penguin Company

2 4 6 8 10 9 7 5 3 1
© LADYBIRD BOOKS LTD MCMXCIV. This edition MMX

LADYBIRD and the device of a Ladybird are trademarks of
Ladybird Books Ltd

ISBN: 978-1-40930-833-1

Printed in China

Ladybird *classics*

PETER PAN

by Sir J. M. Barrie

He listened at nursery windows.

THE BOY WHO
NEVER GREW UP

This is the story of Peter Pan, a boy who ran away to live in the Neverland when he was very young. The Neverland is an island that children visit in their dreams and where anything can happen. To reach it, you have to be able to fly.

Peter could fly. Sometimes, when he felt lonely, he went back to the human world and listened at nursery windows to the bedtime stories mothers told their children.

One of the places Peter especially liked to visit was the nursery window of Wendy, John, and Michael Darling, who lived with their parents near Kensington Gardens in London.

The children had a rather unusual nurse—a big

Newfoundland dog named Nana, who slept in a kennel in the nursery. If she had been on watch the night Peter came, this story would never have happened.

Mrs. Darling was a happy woman, who hugged and kissed her children often. Mr. Darling was more serious. He worried a lot and did not think it was a good idea to have a dog for a nursemaid.

Every night, Mrs. Darling told the children bedtime stories. Then she tucked them in and lit their night-lights. As she tidied up the nursery, she wondered what they were dreaming about.

If Mrs. Darling could have seen into their minds, she would have seen a picture map of the island of Neverland. It had a lagoon, a pirate ship, flamingos, and a coral reef. There was also a forest with wild beasts and fairies.

Mrs. Darling was puzzled because the children talked so much about a boy named Peter Pan, who lived with the fairies. Mr. Darling thought it must be some silly tale Nana had told them. "It all comes from having a dog as a nurse!" he grumbled.

One morning, Mrs. Darling found some leaves just under the nursery window that had not been there the night before. She asked Wendy where they came from. "Peter must have dropped them," Wendy answered. "He's so untidy!"

"How could he get here? It's three floors up," said Mrs. Darling. "You must have been dreaming!"

But Wendy had not been dreaming. The very next night, Mrs. Darling was sewing by the nursery fire and had almost fallen asleep. The window blew open, and a boy dropped in on the floor!

He was dressed all in leaves. A strange little light followed him, darting around the room like a living thing. The light woke Mrs. Darling. She knew at once that the boy was Peter Pan.

She cried out in alarm and Nana bounded into the room and sprang at the boy, who leapt back through the window. Nana closed it, just catching

Peter's shadow by the feet. Nana picked up the shadow and took it to her mistress, who rolled it up and put it in a drawer.

The following Friday, Mr. and Mrs. Darling were invited to a party at a house a few doors away. Mr. Darling and Nana had quarreled earlier that day, so he decided the dog should be chained up in the yard.

Mrs. Darling was worried because Nana kept barking. "That's not her usual bark!" she said. "She only barks like that when there's danger!"

"Nonsense!" said Mr. Darling. "Hurry up, or we'll be late for the party!"

As the front door closed, a bright light flitted in through the nursery window. When the light stood still you could see it was not a light at all, but a fairy. Her name was Tinker Bell.

The next moment Peter himself came through the window. "Come out, Tink, wherever you are," he cried, "and show me where my shadow is!"

It was a fairy named Tinker Bell.

Tinker Bell told him it was in a drawer. Her voice was a golden tinkle, like the chime of tiny bells.

Peter pulled out his shadow and shut the drawer, forgetting that Tinker Bell was still inside. He tried to stick his shadow back on with water, then with soap, but nothing worked. He was in despair when Wendy woke up.

"What's the matter?" she asked.

"My shadow won't stick on!" Peter complained.

"Give it to me," said Wendy. "I'll sew it on!"

Peter was thrilled to have his shadow back, and Wendy was so pleased that she offered him a kiss. Peter, who had never been kissed, thought it must be a present, so he held out his hand. So as not to hurt his feelings, Wendy gave him her thimble. Forever after, he called a kiss a "thimble."

In return for the thimble, Peter gave Wendy an acorn button from his coat. Wendy put it on a chain around her neck. She didn't know it then, but later on that acorn would save her life!

Peter told Wendy all about how he had run away to live with the fairies in Kensington Gardens. Now he lived in the Neverland with the Lost Boys. The Lost Boys were children who had fallen out of their prams when their nurses were not looking. When nobody claimed them, they were sent to the Neverland.

Wendy asked about the fairies.

"Once, a baby's laugh broke into a thousand pieces," explained Peter. "Each piece became a fairy. But now, most children don't believe in fairies. Every time a child says 'I don't believe in fairies,' a fairy somewhere drops down dead!"

Then Peter remembered Tinker Bell, who was still shut in the drawer! He opened the drawer and she zoomed out in a fury, buzzing around the room.

Wendy thought Tink was lovely, but Tinker Bell hated Wendy and was jealous of her. When Peter gave Wendy a "thimble," Tinker Bell gave Wendy's hair a spiteful tug.

FOLLOW ME!

By now Michael and John were awake. Peter told them all about the gang of Lost Boys—of which he was the captain—and their fights with the Pirates.

"Aren't there any Lost Girls?" asked Wendy.

"No," said Peter. "Girls are much too smart to fall out of their prams. So we haven't any mothers to tell us stories or any sisters to play games with us."

"You poor boy!" exclaimed Wendy. "I can tell you lots of stories, and I know ever so many games."

That was just what Peter wanted—to take Wendy and her brothers back to the Neverland with him. He promised to teach them how to fly.

In the yard, Nana was barking like mad. She knew something was wrong. At last, she broke her chain and rushed to the house where the party was going on. She got Mr. and Mrs. Darling, and they all ran down the street as fast as they could.

A moment before, Peter had blown fairy dust all over the children and was now showing them how to fly. "Just wriggle your shoulders and let go!" he cried, swooping around the room. One by one, they took off from their beds and followed him.

"I flewed! I flewed!" shouted Michael.

"Look at me!" called John, bumping against the ceiling. He was wearing his Sunday top hat, and looked very funny.

"Oh, lovely!" cried Wendy, in midair.

Mr. and Mrs. Darling and Nana could see the light from the nursery window. Against the curtains, they saw the shadows of three little figures, circling round and round in the air. No, not three—four!

They rushed upstairs and burst into the room. But they were too late. Peter was shouting, "Follow me!" Then he soared out into the night with John, Michael, and Wendy right behind him.

At last they saw the Neverland below.

THE FLIGHT

Peter said the way to the Neverland was easy: "Second star to the right, and straight on till morning!" But it seemed to take a very long time.

At first flying was fun. The children circled around church spires and raced each other among the clouds. But they eventually grew tired and hungry. Peter stole food for them from the beaks of passing birds, but it was not like a proper meal.

After what seemed to be days and nights, they at last saw the Neverland below. It was just as they had imagined. They saw the lagoon, the mermaids, and the wild beasts.

As they flew down through the treetops, Peter told the children about the Pirates and their dreaded leader, Captain Hook. The children had all heard of him—he was the most bloodthirsty buccaneer who had ever sailed the seven seas.

"I cut off his right hand!" said Peter proudly. "Now he has an iron hook instead, and he uses it like a claw!" The children shivered.

"One thing you have to promise," Peter went on. "If we meet Captain Hook in open fight, you must leave him for me." The children promised.

Just then Tinker Bell flew up, to warn them that the Pirates had loaded their big gun, Long Tom. Tink's light showed the Pirates just where Peter and his friends were flying. So the children hid Tinker Bell in John's top hat, which Wendy carried.

Suddenly there was an enormous BANG! Long Tom had been fired. The blast blew them onto their backs and scattered them across the sky. Tinker Bell and Wendy were separated from the rest.

Tinker Bell was still jealous of Wendy and wanted to get rid of her. So, with her golden tinkle, she led Wendy away in quite the wrong direction.

THE ISLAND
COMES TRUE

Feeling that Peter was coming back, the Neverland came to life. The Lost Boys were out looking for their captain, and the Pirates were out looking for the Lost Boys. The Indians were out looking for the Pirates, and the wild beasts were out looking for the Indians!

There were six Lost Boys: Tootles, the unlucky one; Nibs, the cheerful one; Slightly, the conceited one; Curly, who was always in trouble; and the Twins. They crept along behind the bushes in single file, each one clutching his dagger.

Then came the evil-looking Pirates. Some wore gold earrings, while others were tattooed all over. They had names like Cecco, Bill Jukes, and

17

Gentleman Starkey. The worst one, because he looked so meek and mild, was Smee the Bo'sun. He had a cutlass named Jimmy Corkscrew, which he wriggled in his victims' wounds.

Their leader, Captain Jas. (short for James) Hook, was the most evil rogue of them all. He feared nothing except the sight of his own blood, which was an ugly color. He treated his men like dogs and smoked two cigars at once, in a special holder he had made himself.

Hook had a lean, scowling face and long black ringlets. He thought he looked like King Charles II and tried to dress like him. If any of his crew crossed him, he shot out his hook. There would be a tearing sound, a scream, and then the body would be kicked aside. Hook was Peter's greatest enemy.

The Indians stole along the trail of the Pirates. Their chief was Great Big Little Panther, and Tiger Lily was their princess. She was a proud, beautiful maiden, as brave as any warrior.

Captain Hook was the most evil rogue of all.

Following the Indians came a procession of wild beasts; man-eating lions, bears, and tigers, all with their tongues hanging out. Last of all, there came an enormous crocodile.

All the Lost Boys, except Nibs who stayed to keep watch, escaped to their underground home—a cave hollowed out under the roots of seven tall trees. The trunk of each tree had a door just big enough for a boy to wriggle into. There was one door for each boy, and one for Peter Pan. So far, the Pirates had not discovered them.

Although the Pirates tried to catch Nibs as he ran away, Hook held them back. "One is no good!" he said. "I want all of them!" And he sat down to wait while the Pirates searched the wood.

As he sat, Hook told Smee how Peter Pan had cut off his hand. "He threw it to a passing crocodile," Hook snarled. "It liked the taste so much that it has followed me ever since, licking its lips for the rest of me! Luckily, it also swallowed a clock. It goes *tick,*

tick, tick, so I can hear it coming and escape!"

"One day," said Smee, "that clock will run down!"

"Aye," said Hook, "that's what I'm afraid of."

Just then, a familiar sound reached Hook's ears.

Tick, tick, tick, tick—it was the Crocodile!

Hook and Smee bounded away, and the boys came out of hiding. Nibs rushed back, pointing up at the sky. Something that looked like a great white bird was floating above them. They didn't know that it was actually Wendy in her nightgown.

Tinker Bell was flying all around her, pinching her. Wendy was moaning "Poor Wendy!" to herself.

"Peter wants you to shoot the Wendy bird!" Tink called to the boys.

The boys always did what Peter wanted, so they hurried away for their bows and arrows. Tootles was the first back. "Quick, Tootles, quick!" Tink screamed. "Peter will be so pleased!"

Tootles aimed his bow and fired. Wendy fluttered to the ground, with an arrow in her heart.

"She is dead," said Peter.

THE LITTLE HOUSE
AND THE
HOME UNDERGROUND

When the boys crowded around to see the Wendy bird, they discovered to their horror that it wasn't a bird at all, but a lady.

"A mother to take care of us, at last," said one of the Twins, "and Tootles has shot her."

Poor, unlucky Tootles began to tremble and his face went white. He was about to run away when Peter arrived.

"Good news, boys! I've brought you all a mother," he said joyfully. "Haven't you seen her? She flew this way."

The Lost Boys made no sound, but stood aside and showed him Wendy lying on the ground.

23

"She is dead," said Peter. "Who shot her?"

"I did," Tootles confessed. "Now kill me."

Peter was raising the arrow to strike when Nibs shouted, "The Wendy lady moved her arm!"

"Poor Tootles!" Wendy moaned.

"She's alive!" Peter cried. He knelt down and saw that the acorn button he had given her had stopped the arrow and saved her life.

"Listen to Tink!" said Curly. "She's crying because the Wendy lives."

When the boys told Peter what Tinker Bell had done, Peter was furious. "I am no longer your friend, Tinker Bell," he said. "Go away forever!"

Wendy moved her arm again.

"Well," said Peter, "go away for a week, then."

Tinker Bell wasn't the least bit grateful to Wendy. She just flew away, as cross as two sticks.

The Lost Boys didn't know what they should do to help Wendy. She was too wounded to carry down into the cave.

"I know!" said Peter. "We'll build a little house all around her!"

The boys rushed off to fetch branches, bedding, and firewood, and Michael and John helped.

Bit by bit the house was built, with a green moss carpet, red walls, and a door and windows. At last, all it needed was a chimney. Peter knocked the top out of John's Sunday top hat and fitted it on the roof. It began to smoke at once!

"This is your own little house!" Peter told Wendy.

"And we can be your children!" said the Lost Boys.

The underground cave where Peter and the boys lived was one enormous room. A huge bed hung against the wall and was let down at night. The Lost Boys slept in it like sardines in a tin can.

Wendy and the Lost Boys pretended that she was their mother. Each night she told them a bedtime story, gave them each a goodnight "thimble," and tucked them into their big bed.

The mermaids lazed on the rocks.

THE MERMAIDS' LAGOON

At the edge of the island there was a vivid blue lagoon where mermaids swam. The mermaids lazed on the rocks, combing their long hair and splashing the children with their tails if they came too near. On moonlit nights the mermaids sang strange wailing songs. On those nights it was dangerous for mortals to go near the lagoon.

A Neverbird had once built her nest in one of the trees by the shore and laid six eggs in it. One day the nest fell and floated out on the lagoon. But still the mother bird sat on her eggs, drifting around in her nest as if it were a little boat. Peter gave orders that the Neverbird was not to be disturbed.

In the middle of the lagoon there was a huge

black rock that was covered with water at high tide. The Pirates used to tie their captives to the rock and leave them there to drown, so it was called Marooners' Rock.

One afternoon, when Wendy and the boys were having a nap on the Rock, the sun went in, and the lagoon became cold and unfriendly. Wendy tried not to be afraid, even though she heard the sound of a boat approaching.

Peter, who could smell danger in his sleep, awoke suddenly and cried, "Pirates! Everybody dive!"

The next moment, the Rock was empty.

The pirate dinghy, rowed by Smee and Starkey, drew near. They had captured Tiger Lily as she was boarding the pirate ship with a knife between her teeth. They had tied her hands and feet and were going to leave her on Marooners' Rock to drown. She showed no fear, for she was a chief's daughter.

Peter decided to save Tiger Lily and have some fun at the same time. "Ahoy, you lubbers!" he called, imitating Hook's voice. "Set the Indian free!"

"But Captain," said Smee, "you told us . . ."

"Set her free at once, d'you hear," cried Peter, "or I'll plunge my hook in you!"

"Better do what the Captain orders," muttered Starkey nervously. So they cut Tiger Lily's ropes and she slipped like an eel into the sea.

Suddenly a cry came across the water. "Boat ahoy!" It was the real Captain Hook, swimming out to join his men. He had come to talk about a plan to capture Peter and his gang.

"We may never get the better of those boys now that they have a mother to care for them!" he said.

"I know," said Smee. "But if we capture her, she can be our mother!"

"A capital idea!" cried Hook. "But first we must catch the boys and make them walk the plank!"

Hook was furious to find that his men had let Tiger Lily go. "I gave no such orders!" he said.

When they told him about the mysterious voice,

Hook was frightened. "Spirit that haunts this dark lagoon," he called, "dost thou hear me?"

Peter could not keep quiet. "Odds, bobs, hammer and tongs, I hear you!" he called.

"Who are you, stranger?" asked Hook hoarsely.

"I am James Hook, Captain of the *Jolly Roger!*"

"If you are Hook, then who am I?"

"You are a codfish!"

Hook went pale at this insult. He knew now who was playing this trick on him. "Are you a boy?" he called. "Are you a *wonderful* boy?"

"Yes, yes!" boasted Peter. "I am! I'm Peter Pan!"

At once Hook ordered his men to attack. "Take him, dead or alive!" he cried.

Peter whistled to the boys, and they all came to his aid, armed with daggers. They put up a good fight. Before long, Smee and Starkey were swimming for their lives toward the pirate ship.

Peter had ordered the boys to leave Hook to him, so they rowed to shore in the pirate dinghy.

They put up a good fight.

Peter and Hook came out of the water at the same moment. They stared grimly at each other as they climbed onto the Rock, and Peter snatched a knife from Hook's belt. Then, seeing that Hook was lower down than he was, Peter gave him a hand up, so they could fight fairly. But the villainous Hook bit Peter's hand. Peter was thrown off guard, so Hook was able to claw him twice.

The tide was rising rapidly, so Hook struck out for his ship, leaving Peter on Marooners' Rock, too wounded to swim to shore. As the tide rose, Peter's heart beat like a drum. A strange smile came over his face, and he thought, "To die will be an awfully big adventure!"

But Peter did not die. The Neverbird came by in her nest and rescued him. When he returned to the cave, he saw campfires outside. The Indians had come to protect the boys from a Pirate attack. Since Peter had saved Tiger Lily, there was nothing they would not do for him and his friends.

WENDY'S STORY

Safe inside their cave, the children gathered around Wendy as she prepared to tell them a bedtime story.

She began to tell a story that Peter hated. It was about three children who had a nurse named Nana, and how they flew away one night, and how their father and mother missed them. "Think how sad their parents were when they saw the empty beds!" she said.

Then she came to the part that Peter hated most. She told the boys how much mothers love their children. "The mother always left the window open waiting for her children to fly back in. So they stayed away for years and had a lovely time."

Peter was very upset. "Wendy, you're wrong

about mothers!" he said. Then he told them what had happened when he went back home. "Long ago, I thought, like you, that my mother would always keep the window open for me. So I stayed away a long time. But when I flew back, my mother had forgotten me. The window was shut, and there was another little boy in my bed!"

Michael and John began to cry, afraid that their mother might forget them too. They begged Wendy to take them home. The Lost Boys said they wanted to come too, and Wendy promised she would ask Mr. and Mrs. Darling to adopt them.

Peter was very hurt, but he was too proud to show it. And he would not make Wendy stay in the Neverland against her will. "I will ask the Indians to show you the way through the wood, and Tinker Bell can guide you when you fly over the sea," he said casually.

"But aren't you coming too?" asked Wendy.

"Oh, no!" exclaimed Peter. "They would make

They begged Wendy to take them home.

me grow up! I want to stay a little boy always, and have fun!"

Then Peter and Wendy shook hands—Peter did not even give Wendy a "thimble." Wendy measured out a dose of his medicine (which was really only water), and put the glass next to his bed. "Promise me you'll take it, Peter," she said in a motherly way.

"I promise," answered Peter, who was not about to cry in front of the others. "Now lead the way, Tinker Bell!" he ordered.

Tink darted up the nearest tree, but nobody followed her. For it was at that moment that the Pirates made their dreadful attack on the Indians. The air above the cave was full of shrieks and howls and the clash of steel!

Below, there was dead silence. Wendy fell to her knees, and the boys turned to Peter, holding out their arms and begging him not to desert them.

Peter seized his trusty sword, ready to do battle.

THE CHILDREN ARE
CARRIED OFF

Hook and his fiendish crew had taken the
Indians by surprise, so the Pirates had an unfair
advantage. Almost the whole Indian tribe perished.
Only the chief, Tiger Lily, and a few warriors
managed to fight their way out and survive.

But Hook's work was not over yet. There was
hatred in his wicked heart for Peter Pan.

Hook knew that if the boys heard the Indians'
tom-tom, they would come out of hiding, thinking
the Indians had won. So he signaled to Smee, who
beat the tom-tom twice.

"It's an Indian victory!" cried Peter.

The boys cheered and got ready to leave the cave,
saying a last good-bye to Peter.

But as they came up they were caught, one by one, by the Pirates, who tied them up like chickens.

Then the Pirates bundled the children into the little Wendy house and carried it on their shoulders to the *Jolly Roger*.

Hook stayed behind in the woods. He looked carefully at the trees and discovered that one of them was more hollow than the others and he could just squeeze inside. He could not open the door, but he peered through a crack and saw Peter lying peacefully asleep on the great bed. For a moment his cold heart was touched. Then he spied Peter's medicine, which he could just reach.

Hook always carried a deadly poison in his pocket. Reaching through the crack, he poured five drops into Peter's medicine.

Then he climbed out of the tree like an evil spirit. Pulling his hat over his eyes, he wrapped his black cloak around him and stole away through the forest, back to the *Jolly Roger*.

They were caught, one by one, by the Pirates.

DO YOU BELIEVE
IN FAIRIES?

At ten o'clock that night, Peter was awakened by a tiny knock on the door. It was Tinker Bell, who told him that Wendy and the boys had been captured and taken to the Pirate ship.

"I'll rescue them!" cried Peter, grabbing his sword. "But first I must take my medicine!"

"No! No!" cried Tinker Bell. "It's poisoned!"

"How could it be?" said Peter. "Nobody has been down here." He put the glass to his lips. But brave Tinker Bell had heard Hook boasting to himself in the forest that he had poisoned Peter Pan, so she flew between Peter's mouth and the glass. She drank the poison herself, in one gulp.

"It was poisoned!" she cried. "Now I shall die!"

She fluttered feebly to her tiny couch and lay there gasping. Her light was getting weaker every moment. Soon it would go out.

Tink was whispering something. Peter bent down to listen. "If enough children believe in fairies," she gasped, "I might get better again!"

What could Peter do? It was the middle of the night, and children everywhere were asleep. Then he thought of those who were dreaming of Neverland. He called, "If you believe in fairies, clap your hands! Don't let Tink die!"

There was silence. Then there was a faint sound of clapping. It grew and grew until it filled the cave. Tink was saved! Her voice grew strong and she flashed around the room, as merry as ever.

"And now to rescue Wendy!" cried Peter.

He came up through the tree into the moonlit wood. He heard no sound and saw no living thing, except the Crocodile, which never slept.

Peter swore an oath: "It's Hook or me this time!"

"Have you any last message for your children?"

THE FIGHT ON THE
PIRATE SHIP

Aboard the *Jolly Roger*, Hook had the boys dragged up from the hold. He promised to spare two of them if they would join the crew.

"Would we be respectful subjects of the King?" asked John, bravely.

"You would have to swear 'Down with the King!'" Hook growled through his teeth.

"Then we say No!" was the answer.

"Bring out the plank!" roared Hook. "And fetch their mother!"

Wendy was brought up to see her boys walk to their death in the deadly waves of the ocean.

"Have you any last message for your children?" sneered Hook.

Wendy spoke out firmly, "All your mothers hope you will die bravely like true Englishmen!"

"Tie her to the mast!" Hook screamed.

The boys' eyes were on the plank—the last walk they would ever take. At last the grim silence was broken by a strange sound, the *tick, tick, tick* of the Crocodile!

Hook collapsed with fear. He crawled along the deck, crying to his men, "Hide me! Hide me!"

As the crew gathered around Hook, the boys looked over the side and saw—not the Crocodile, but Peter Pan! He was ticking! Signaling to the boys not to give him away, he slipped aboard and ran to hide in the Captain's cabin.

When the ticking stopped, Hook grew brave again. He lined up the boys for a flogging and sent Jukes to his cabin for the cat-o'-nine-tails.

Jukes entered the dark room. Suddenly there was a terrible scream followed by a blood-chilling crow. Jukes had been killed by Peter!

Two more Pirates suffered the same fate.

After this, none of the terrified crew would venture forth. So Hook sent in the eight boys. "Let them kill each other!" he snarled.

This was just what Peter wanted. He unlocked the boys' chains with a key he had found, and armed them with Hook's weapons. Then, while the Pirates' backs were turned, they all crept out on deck. Peter freed Wendy and, wrapping himself in her cloak, took her place at the mast. Then he let out a terrific "Cock-a-doodle-doo!"

The Pirates, frightened out of their wits, spun around. "'Tis an unlucky ship," they cried, "that has a captain with a hook!"

"'Tis because we have a woman on board," said Hook quickly. "Fling Wendy overboard!"

"No one can save you now, missy!" hissed one of the Pirates jeeringly.

"Here's one who can!" cried Peter, throwing aside the cloak. "Peter Pan!"

A great fight began. Swords clashed, and bodies tumbled into the water. Soon only Hook was left. The boys surrounded him. Hook's sword, flashing like a circle of fire, kept them at bay.

"Leave him to me, boys!" cried Peter.

Peter was nimble and soon wounded Hook. At the sight of his own blood, which was a gruesome color, Hook turned pale and dropped his sword. He rushed to set fire to the powder kegs and blow up the ship. But Peter bravely snatched the torch from his hand and threw it into the sea.

Hook backed away from Peter and climbed onto the bulwark. Peter kicked him, and Hook lost his balance, and fell into the water.

The Crocodile, whose clock had run down at last, had silently followed Peter and was waiting patiently below. It finally had the rest of Hook for its supper.

"Leave him to me, boys!"

THE RETURN HOME

That night the boys slept in the Pirates' bunks, and the next morning they set sail for home, with Peter as captain.

Meanwhile, Mr. and Mrs. Darling were still grieving over their lost children. Mr. Darling was sure it was all his fault for chaining up Nana, and, to punish himself, he slept in her kennel in the nursery.

One night, he was feeling especially miserable, so he asked Mrs. Darling to play the piano in the room next door to cheer him up. "And please shut the window," he said. "It's drafty in the nursery."

"You know I can't do that, dear!" said Mrs. Darling. "The children might come home!"

But the children were already on their way!

48

They had crossed the sea and were flying the last leg of the journey. Peter and Tinker Bell flew ahead of the others. When they found the open window and flew in, Peter planned to shut the window so that Wendy would think her mother had forgotten her, and go back with him to the Neverland.

But Mrs. Darling was sitting sadly at the piano, with tears trickling down her face.

"She is fond of Wendy too!" thought Peter miserably. "We can't both have her. What should I do?" Finally he gave in and said, "Oh, come on, Tink. We'll let them in."

So Wendy and Michael and John slipped into the nursery. They climbed into bed and pretended they had never been away.

When Mrs. Darling came in and saw that the beds were full, she thought it was a dream! Then the children spoke to her. She put her arms around them, woke her husband, and called Nana.

Peter Pan had had many fantastic adventures that

He was looking at the one joy he would never share.

other children would never know, but now he was looking through the window at the one joy he could never share.

The Darlings adopted the Lost Boys, and Mrs. Darling let Wendy go back to the Neverland once a year to help Peter with the spring-cleaning.

Peter was to supposed to come back and fetch Wendy. But time meant so little to him, he did not come every year. Once, he didn't return for so long that when he finally came, Wendy was grown up and had a little girl of her own, named Jane.

Since Wendy was now too old to fly, she let Jane go back to the Neverland with Peter.

Peter never grew up, so one year Jane's *daughter* was the one who went. And so it will go on, as long as there are children, and the Neverland, and Peter Pan!